Dear Barbie™

Best Friends

Written by Mary Packard
Illustrated by S. I. Artists

A Golden Book • New York
Western Publishing Company, Inc., Racine, Wisconsin 53404

Dear Barbie,

I am in first grade and my best friend lives across the street from me. There is another girl from school who was very good friends with my best friend last year in kindergarten. It is really hard because this girl and I fight over my best friend. She tries to make my best friend play with only her on the playground.

Has this ever happened to you?

Love,
Emily

$\mathcal{B}$arbie sat down to answer Emily's letter. She wrote:

> Dear Emily,
>   This reminds me of the time I carpooled three
> girls to gymnastics and they couldn't get along.

Barbie continued her letter to Emily. And this is the story she told. . . .

One afternoon Susan, Kristen, and Jennifer were getting ready for gymnastics. Barbie called, "Hurry, girls. We don't want to be late."

"*I can't wait to practice on the low beam with Kristen,*" thought Jennifer.

At the gym, the coach announced, "Just two more weeks until the big meet. Now, let's start practicing!"

Susan quickly took Kristen's arm and headed for the mat.

"Can I come, too?" asked Jennifer.

"Kristen and I are partners today," said Susan.

"I can do a split," bragged Susan. "Kristen, look at me!"

"That's great," replied Kristen. Jennifer felt like crying and tried to hold back her tears.

At the end of practice, Jennifer waved good-bye to the coach.

"Ex-cuuuse me!" giggled Susan as she bumped into Jennifer.

"*She did that on purpose!*" thought Jennifer.

Barbie noticed that Jennifer was quiet on the ride home.

"Is something wrong?" asked Barbie as she waved good-bye to the others.

"Yes, Kristen is *my* friend, but today she only practiced with Susan," said Jennifer. "And Susan wasn't very nice."

"It's hard when there are three friends," said Barbie.
"Sometimes someone feels left out, and feelings can get
hurt."

Barbie and Jennifer continued to talk.

Jennifer thought about what Barbie said in the car. At the next week's practice, Jennifer decided she would train with someone else.

"Beth, want to go on the low beam?" asked Jennifer.

"Sure," replied Beth.

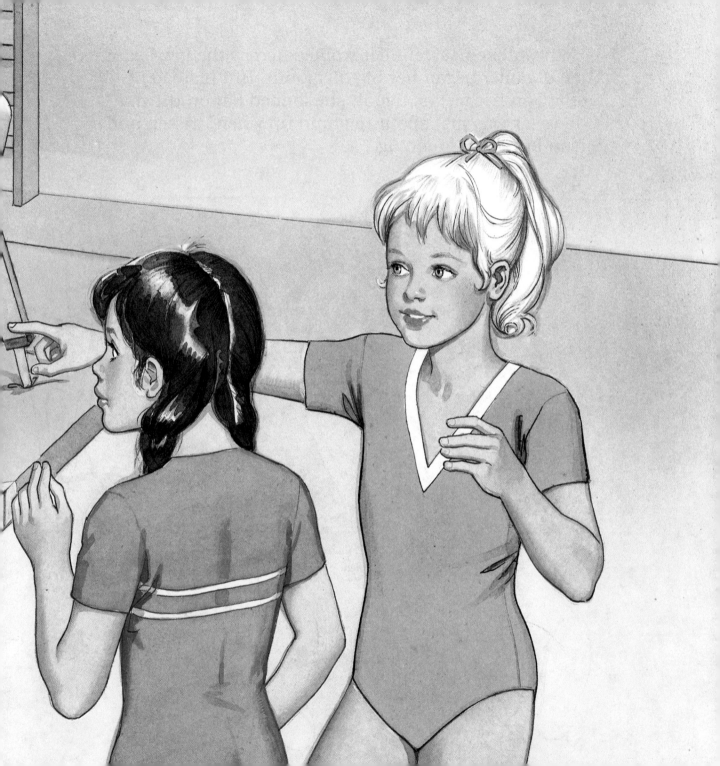

Beth watched as Jennifer walked across the low beam. Then Jennifer began her big dismount. But instead of landing on her feet as usual, she landed flat on the mat!

Jennifer was just about to stand up when Kristen and Susan burst out laughing.

That was the last straw! Jennifer ran off to the locker room in tears.

"We always laugh when we goof," Kristen said, looking puzzled. "I'd better go see what's wrong."

"But I'm up next," said Susan. "Wait until after my routine."

"No," replied Kristen. "I have to see if Jennifer's okay."

"What's wrong?" asked Kristen.

"You're supposed to be my best friend, so why are you spending all your time with Susan?" said Jennifer.

"I am your best friend," replied Kristen. "But I also like Susan."

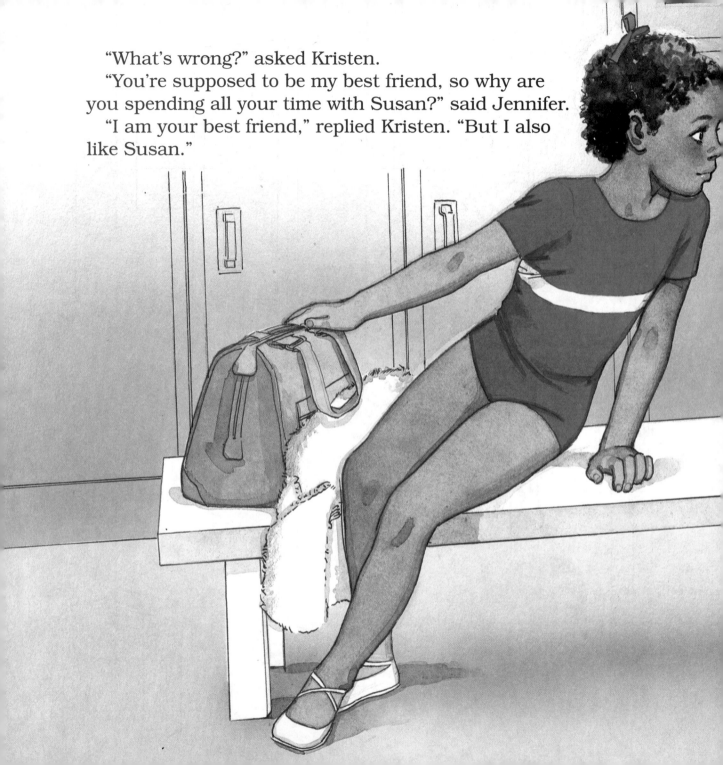

Just then Barbie walked in and offered some advice.

"Maybe you could practice with Kristen one session and with Beth the next session," suggested Barbie.

"That works for me," said Jennifer.

"Me, too!" replied Kristen as they happily headed back to the gym.

It was finally the day of the big meet. Jennifer began
her dismount and landed perfectly on her feet!

"Way to go, Jennifer!" shouted Susan.

"We did it!" said Kristen, jumping up and down. "We won the championship!"

"I'm so proud of you girls," said Barbie.

Barbie finished her letter to Emily:

You see, being best friends isn't always easy. Sometimes you'll disagree, but you can work it out. And don't forget, you can always make new friends, too!

Love,
Barbie

Stories from real girls with real solutions!

What do you do when your best friend starts playing with someone else? Ask Barbie! That's what Emily did. In *Best Friends*, will Barbie be able to help Emily realize that three isn't always a crowd?

Dear Barbie™ books delicately address some of the issues that young children face today. With a little help from Barbie, readers will learn positive solutions to very common situations.

Special Edition

59758-00